First published in Great Britain 2023 by Farshore
An imprint of HarperCollins*Publishers*,
1 London Bridge Street, London SE1 9GF
www.farshore.co.uk

HarperCollins*Publishers* Macken House, 39/40 Mayor Street Upper, Dublin 1, D01 C9W8, Ireland

Written by Laura Jackson.

© 2023 Disney Enterprises, Inc.

ISBN 978 0 00 853718 0
Printed in China
2

A CIP catalogue record for this title is available from the British Library.

Parental guidance is advised for all craft and colouring activities. Always ask an adult to help
when using glue, paint and scissors. Wear protective clothing and cover surfaces to avoid staining.

Stay safe online. Farshore is not responsible for content hosted by third parties.

Farshore takes its responsibility to the planet and its inhabitants very seriously.
We aim to use papers from well-managed forests run by responsible suppliers.

This Disney
FROZEN
ANNUAL 2024

Belongs to . . . .

. . . .

Age . . . .

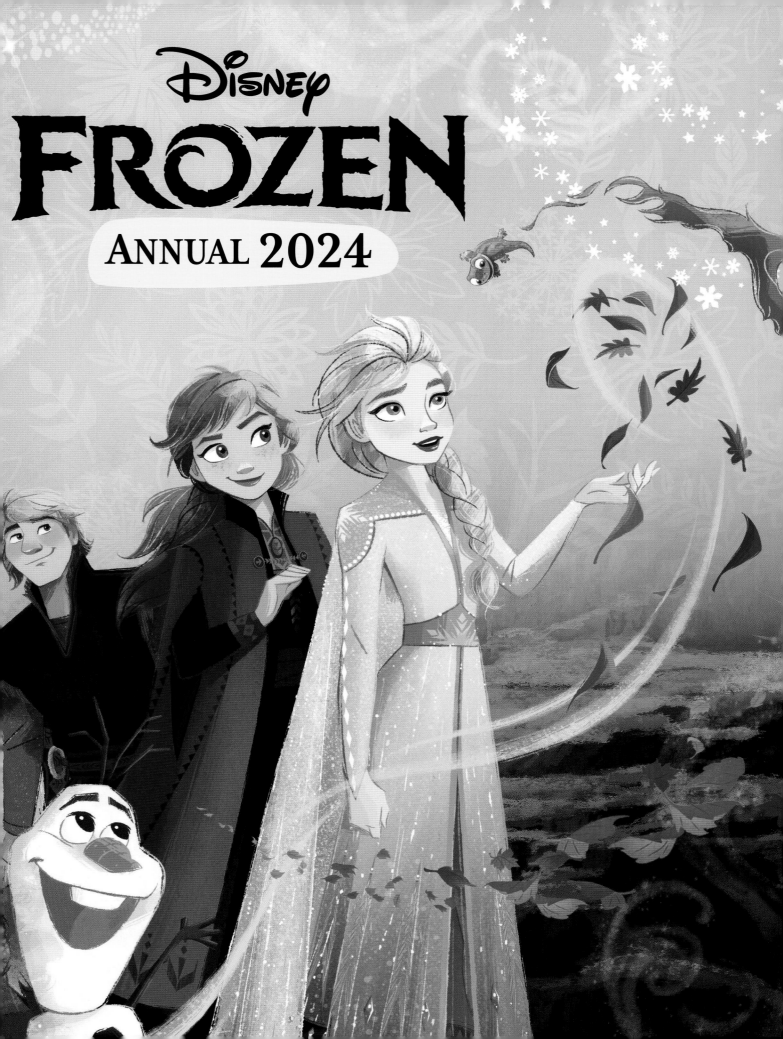

Contents

A Frozen World

Friendship, adventure, nature and magic unite the people of Arendelle and Northuldra. Follow the leaves to meet the friends and discover their strengths.

MAGIC

ADVENTURE

Anna

Anna has a big heart and loves to be busy! She hops from one adventure to the next, taking her friends along for the ride.

Elsa

Born with magic to control snow and ice, Elsa used to hide her powers. Now she is proud to be her true self.

WARM HUGS

Olaf

Happy and full of hugs, Olaf is one loveable little snowman. And now he can read, he wants to tell everyone just how clever he is!

Kristoff

This tough ice harvester was brought up by trolls. He loves being outside with his reindeer Sven, but Anna soon melts his heart.

FRIENDSHIP

Sven

Wherever Kristoff goes, Sven goes too. This trusty sidekick is not afraid of danger when it comes to helping his best bud.

NATURE

REINDEER

Yelana

Yelana is the leader of the Northuldra. Nature guides her and she listens to the powers of the Enchanted Forest.

Ryder

Ryder loves reindeer, so it's no surprise he makes fast friends with Kristoff. Ryder loves his family too, but he dreams of adventures outside the magical mist.

HELPFUL

Honeymaren

Honeymaren is an expert tree climber and reindeer rider. She is super smart and helps Elsa find the truth of the past.

Adventure Ready

Anna is about to go on a mission into the unknown. Draw three things Anna could take on her journey.

Anna could bring:
- A map • A rope • A scarf

Make a Change

Look at Elsa's swirling, whirling snowy magic! She has made a secret change to one of these pictures. Can you find the odd one out?

a

b

c

d

e

f

Answers on page 69.

Special Seasons

Olaf loves jumping in crunchy leaves in autumn. Elsa likes icy winter days best. Use the colour chart to help you decorate the trees, just for Olaf and Elsa.

Autumn Colours

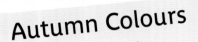

Winter Colours

Say three things out loud that you love about autumn or winter.

Nature is Magic

In the Enchanted Forest, magic is everywhere. Four powerful spirits represent fire, water, earth and wind. Follow the trails to match each spirit with their power.

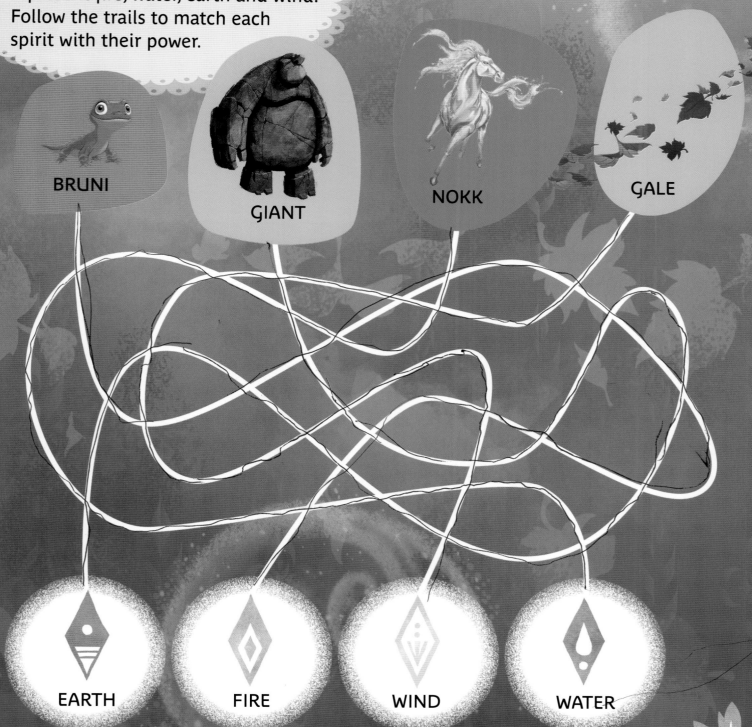

BRUNI

GIANT

NOKK

GALE

EARTH

FIRE

WIND

WATER

Answers on page 69.

The Mystery Hunt

Script by Valentina Cambi; layout: Emilio Urbano; cleanup: Letizia Algeri; colour: MAAWillustration

IT'S A NEW SEASON...

THE TAILOR IS HERE, YOUR MAJESTY!

GOOD MORNING!

COME IN, HILDE!

HOW CAN I HELP YOU?

I BET SOMEONE COULD USE THESE DRESSES, SO I'D LIKE YOU TO TURN THEM INTO OUTFITS FOR PEOPLE WHO NEED NEW CLOTHES!

THAT'S A WONDERFUL IDEA, YOUR MAJESTY! I'LL DO MY BEST!

THANK YOU! I'LL COME BY LATER AFTER I FINISH CHOOSING THEM...

TAKE MY BUTTONS! THE TAILOR CAN USE THEM, TOO!

YOU HAVE SUCH A BIG HEART, OLAF! BUT YOU CAN KEEP THEM...

I'M SURE ELSA WOULD BE HAPPY TO DONATE HER OLD CLOTHES, TOO...

SO...

THESE CLOTHES BRING BACK SO MANY MEMORIES!

DO YOU KNOW WHAT I MISS THE MOST?

WARM HUGS?

OF COURSE, OLAF! BUT I WAS ALSO THINKING OF...

... OUR MOTHER'S SCARF!

LET'S GO GET IT! I KEEP IT IN MY TRUNK!

NO PROBLEM, THE TRUNK IS IN MY WORKSHOP! IT'S THIS WAY!

BUT...

HOW STRANGE... I THOUGHT I CLOSED IT!

?!

THE SCARF... IS MISSING!

I'M VERY SORRY! I DON'T KNOW WHAT HAPPENED...

DO YOU KNOW IF SOMEONE MIGHT HAVE TAKEN THE SCARF?

KRISTINE, MY DAUGHTER! SHE'S ALWAYS PLAYING HERE...

SHE JUST LEFT FOR THE FJORD TO PLAY WITH FRIENDS!

WE NEED TO FIND HER!

DON'T WORRY, ANNA! DETECTIVE OLAF IS HERE!

DETECTIVE OLAF IMMEDIATELY GETS TO WORK!

WHAT DOES KRISTINE LOOK LIKE?

SHE HAS BLUE EYES AND LONG BLOND HAIR GATHERED IN A BRAID... SHE'S NOT VERY TALL, AND SHE HAS A SUNNY SMILE!

LET'S GO! WE'VE GOT HER PORTRAIT.

HA HA!

BUT WHEN THEY ARRIVE AT THE FJORD'S SHORE...

I BELIEVE IN YOU, DETECTIVE OLAF!

OH, DEAR! THIS IS GOING TO BE HARDER THAN I THOUGHT!

HI! ARE YOU KRISTINE?

NO, I'M BRITT!

MY NAME IS CAMILLA! AND YOU?

I'M NOT KRISTINE, EITHER! THANK YOU. BYE, FRIENDS!

UH?!

THE SEARCH CONTINUES...

EXCUSE ME! DO YOU HAPPEN TO KNOW THE TAILOR'S DAUGHTER?

SORRY, YOUR MAJESTY, WE DON'T!

WHAT DO I SEE HERE: CUTE LITTLE DOLL CLOTHES! WHO MADE THEM?

MY MUM!

SHE MUST BE A VERY GOOD TAILOR!

OH, YES! EVERYONE THINKS SO, EVEN THE QUEEN!

YOUR MAJESTY!

HI! IS YOUR NAME KRISTINE?

YES! HOW CAN I HELP YOU?

HEE HEE! DETECTIVE OLAF NEVER FAILS...

KRISTINE, DID YOU HAPPEN TO TAKE A SCARF FROM YOUR MUM'S WORKSHOP THIS MORNING?

EHM, I DID... IT WAS SO WARM AND COMFORTABLE!

Continued on page 30 ...

19

A New World

Beyond the dark mist, the friends have found a forest alive with magic and secrets. It's time to explore! Can you spot 5 differences in picture 2 before the adventure begins?

1

Colour in a leaf each time you spot a difference.

2

Answers on page 69.

Best Buds

Sven, Olaf and Kristoff are like one fun, snowy, happy family! Can you find the matching pair of pictures?

1

2

3

4

5

6

Answers on page 69.

The Greatest Bond

Friends and family are everything to Anna. Now it's time to meet the people that make you happy. Draw pictures of the special people and pets (or snowmen!) in your life.

Say out loud one kind or funny thing about each person you've drawn.

Shield of Nature

Mattias is very proud of his Arendelle shield. Can you design your own shield of nature? Draw your favourite parts of nature in each section. Use the ideas box to help you.

Ideas Box

Tick ✔ the four parts of nature you love best and draw them in each part of your shield.

- ☑ Animals
- ☑ Trees
- ☐ Flowers
- ☐ Sea
- ☐ Mountains
- ☐ Snow
- ☐ Rainbows
- ☐ Sun

Troll Trails

When Kristoff and Anna need help, they know exactly who to ask – wise, old Grand Pabbie! All the excited little trolls are ready to show them the way. Use the key to follow the correct pattern of trolls, all the way to Grand Pabbie.

Follow this key:

Answers on page 69.

Party Prep

Olaf needs your help, and fast! He has forgotten to finish half of Anna's birthday cake, and the party starts in **two minutes**. Quickly set a timer, grab your crayons and get cake decorating.

True or False?

Are you a Frozen snow-it-all with an un-brrr-lievable memory? Take the quiz to find out! Circle your answers.

1. Olaf is a snow monster. — True / False

2. Anna has five troll brothers. — True / False

3. A mist covers the Enchanted Forest. — True / False

4. Ryder doesn't like reindeer. — True / False

5. Yelana is the leader of the Northuldra. — True / False

6. Arendelle Castle is made of rainbows. — True / False

7. Sven can fly. — True / False

8. Olaf loves reading books. — True / False

9. Kristoff was brought up by trolls. — True / False

10. Elsa and Anna are twins. — True / False

How did you do?

1–4 N-ice try!

5–7 Thaw-some work!

8–10 You snow everything!

Giant Dash

Watch out, the Earth Giants are grumpy and rumbly today. Use a pencil to guide Anna to Kristoff. But ssshhh, go slowly. If you bump into the sides, the giants might see you and you will have to start again!

START

FINISH

Winter Wonderland

What sparkling magic is Elsa creating in the Enchanted Forest? Connect the numbered crystals to find out.

1

20

2

17

18

19

3

16

4

5

15

6

14

7

11

8

12

13

10

9

Answers on page 69.

Script by Valentina Cambi; layout: Emilio Urbano; cleanup: Letizia Algeri; colour: MAAWillustration

ANNA, ELSA AND OLAF HAVE JUST FOUND KRISTINE...

THAT SCARF IS REALLY SPECIAL. IT BELONGED TO OUR MOTHER!

DO YOU HAVE IT WITH YOU?

NOT ANYMORE! I GAVE IT TO AN **OLD WOMAN** WHO WAS COLD, TOO!

I'M SORRY!

IT'S OKAY! DON'T WORRY!

IT WAS VERY KIND OF YOU TO SHARE IT!

DO YOU KNOW WHERE THE WOMAN LIVES?

NO, I HAD NEVER SEEN HER BEFORE...

THANKS ANYWAY, KRISTINE! KEEP PLAYING WITH YOUR FRIENDS!

I'M AFRAID WE'VE LOST THE SCARF FOREVER, ANNA!

WE'LL FIND IT, ELSA! I PROMISE!

THESE FOOTPRINTS MUST BELONG TO THE MYSTERY WOMAN! LET'S FOLLOW THEM!

HOW DID YOU FIGURE THAT OUT?

SHE PROBABLY USES A CANE! THAT'S WHY ONE OF THE HOLES IS SMALLER...

ANNA, ELSA AND OLAF ARRIVE AT A LITTLE COTTAGE...

GOOD MORNING!

GOOD MORNING, YOUR MAJESTY! PLEASE COME IN!

IS THERE SOMETHING I CAN HELP YOU WITH?

WE'RE LOOKING FOR A SPECIAL SCARF...

SO IT'S YOUR SCARF THAT KEPT ME SO WARM!

WHEN I WENT OUT THIS MORNING, I DIDN'T REALISE IT WAS COLD... FORTUNATELY, THAT LITTLE GIRL HELPED ME!

IF YOU NEED THE SCARF, PLEASE KEEP IT!

WE'RE HAPPY TO KNOW IT MAKES YOU FEEL PROTECTED AND COMFORTABLE!

I CAN COME HERE EVERY DAY TO GIVE YOU **WARM HUGS!**

YOU'RE SO KIND, BUT I HAVE MY OWN SHAWL AND EVERYTHING AT HOME TO STAY WARM!

I CAN TELL THAT SCARF IS REALLY PRECIOUS. YOU MUST HAVE IT BACK!

PLEASE COME WITH ME! IT'S IN MY BEDROOM!

THANK YOU SO MUCH!

AND...

HERE IT IS!

FINALLY!

ANNA PROMPTLY USES THE SCARF LIKE A LASSO...

YAHA!

THAT WAS CLOSE!

GREAT MOVE, ANNA!

YEAHHH!

I LOVE YOU!

ME TOO!

I'M SO HAPPY WE FOUND YOUR MUM'S SCARF!

THANKS FOR YOUR HELP, DETECTIVE OLAF! WHAT I'M HAPPIEST ABOUT IS THE SCARF GAVE A BIT OF COMFORT TO OTHER PEOPLE AS WELL!

VERY TRUE, ANNA! THAT IS ITS REAL GIFT!

The End

35

Into the Unknown

The Enchanted Forest is full of danger and secrets, but the friends are determined to journey into the unknown. Can you be the first to make it through the forest to Elsa?

You will need:
- a dice
- counters (coins, paper, toy figures)
- 2–4 players

Anna

Honeymaren

START 1
2
4
5
7
9
10
11
13
14
15
17
18
FINISH 20
19

START 1
3
4
6
7
8
9
11
12
13
15
17

How to play:

- Choose a character and take turns to throw the dice.
- Move forward the number of spaces shown.
- The first player to Elsa wins!

If you land on Gale, you get blown back **1** space.

If you land on the Water Nokk, gallop forward **2** spaces.

If you land on an Earth Giant, go back to the start!

If you land on Bruni, ask another player to move back **1** space.

Elsa

Kristoff

Olaf

START
1
2
3
5

4
2
START
1

5
7
9
10
12
13
15
16
18
19
FINISH 20

13
14
12
16
10
17
8
18
7
FINISH 20
FINISH 20

Castle Designs

Anna and Elsa are proud to open up their castle to the people of Arendelle. Connect the dots to magic up your own castle.

Colour in your design to make it unique. Doodle flowers, windows, doors, fun patterns ... anything you like!

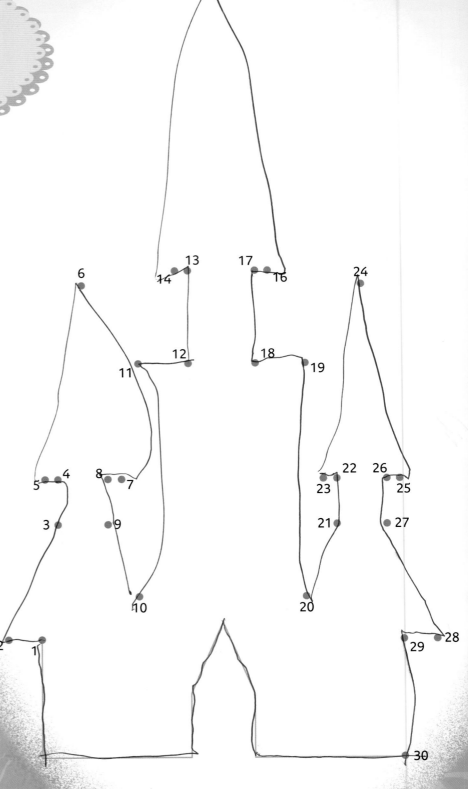

Snow Kind

Being kind is cool. Olaf, Anna and Elsa are always kind to each other and to everyone they meet.

1
Hug someone.

2
Make your friends laugh!

3
Write a letter to a friend.

4
Make your friend smile with a silly song!

5
Make something for your friends.

6
Give your friend a high-5!

Can you play along with Olaf's 'Snow Kind' game? Simply roll a dice, find the matching number on the snowflake and take the challenge.

The Lost Toys

Adapted from *The Great Ice Engine* written by Erica David; Manuscript adaptation by: Chantal Pericoli; Layout: Emilio Urbano; Clean: Manuela Razzi; Colour: Stefania Santi

YEARS AGO, IN THE ARENDELLE CASTLE...

DO I HAVE TO, ELSA?

YES, ANNA.

BUT CAN'T I DO IT LATER?

MAMA SAID ONCE YOU'RE FINISHED, WE CAN GO PLAY IN THE SNOW.

I JUST WISH THERE WAS A FASTER WAY TO DO THIS.

MAYBE... HEY! I HAVE AN IDEA.

A FEW MINUTES LATER...

THAT END IS TOO HEAVY, ELSA...

THUD

I KNOW... BUT WATCH THIS.

HAND ME THAT ROPE...

DO I GET TO SEESAW?

NOT YOU... THEM!

The End

43

Secret Shadows

A mysterious mist covers the Enchanted Forest. Can you work out who is who from their misty shadows?

Answers on page 69.

Blowing a Gale

Whoosh! Gusty Gale has blown Olaf into pieces. Guide Kristoff through the forest maze to pick up Olaf, piece by piece.

When you have collected up Olaf, draw in the pieces to make him whole again!

Group Chat

It's noisy in Arendelle today. Everybody is talking at once. Who is saying what? Match up the words to the friends.

Let it go! Let it go!

Do you want to build a snowman?

Some people are worth melting for.

Reindeer are better than people.

Olaf

Kristoff

Elsa

Anna

Sven doesn't use words, but what do you think he would say if he could talk?

....
....
....
....

Answers on page 69.

Friendship Forever

The magic of friendship is powerful. Together, friends can do anything! Use your crayons to colour in the picture.

Draw in more leaves.

Snow-it-all

Olaf is learning to read. He has just found some fun words that are all about him. Start at the big dots and trace over Olaf's special words.

kind

hugs

fun

snow

Say out loud three words all about YOU!

Strong Spirits

Trust Your Journey

Elsa is ready to use all her powers to journey across the Dark Sea. Guide her safely through the stormy waves to the Water Nokk. Stay away from whirlpools and jagged rocks along the way!

Answers on page 69.

Dragon Days

Adapted from *Anna & Elsa: The Secret Admirer* written by Erica David; Manuscript adaptation by: Steve Behling; Layout: Marino Gentile; Clean: Marino Gentile; Ink and Colour: MAAwillustration

IT'S THE PERFECT DAY FOR A WALK IN THE FORESTS OF ARENDELLE!

I LOVE THE FOREST!

YOU DO?

WHY'S THAT?

I FEEL LIKE THE TREES JUST GET ME!

SUDDENLY...

CLANK CLANK CLANK

WHAT'S THAT NOISE?!

IT'S COMING FROM OVER THERE!

STAY HERE — I'LL INVESTIGATE!

OLAF...

CRASH

MAYBE IT'S MARSHMALLOW, JUST HAVING SOME FUN!

OR KRISTOFF, DROPPING A GIANT STACK OF POTS AND PANS BECAUSE HE'S CLUMSY!

CLANK

CRASH

SINCE WHEN DOES KRISTOFF CARRY AROUND POTS AND PANS?

SINCE WHEN IS KRISTOFF CLUMSY?

HMMMM...

THEN MAYBE IT'S A BAND! BANGING CYMBALS TOGETHER! THEY'RE FAR AWAY ON THE MOUNTAIN AND THE ECHOES TRAVEL A GIGANTIC DISTANCE!

REMIND YOU OF ANYONE, ELSA?

US, WE PLAYED GAMES LIKE THAT WHEN WE WERE LITTLE!

WHAT DO YOU SAY, WE GIVE HIM A SURPRISE?

I SAY...YES!

I SAY YES, TOO! I LIKE SAYING YES!

WHAT DID YOU HAVE IN MIND?

A LITTLE SOMETHING...

...LIKE...

...THIS!

THAT'S PERFECT!

EEEEP!

Better Together

Anna and Elsa have been through good times and bad times, but they are always stronger together. Colour in this picture before the sisters set off on an epic adventure.

So Many Brunis!

Bruni is playing tricks again. Can you spot and circle the three Brunis from the panel hiding in the big picture?

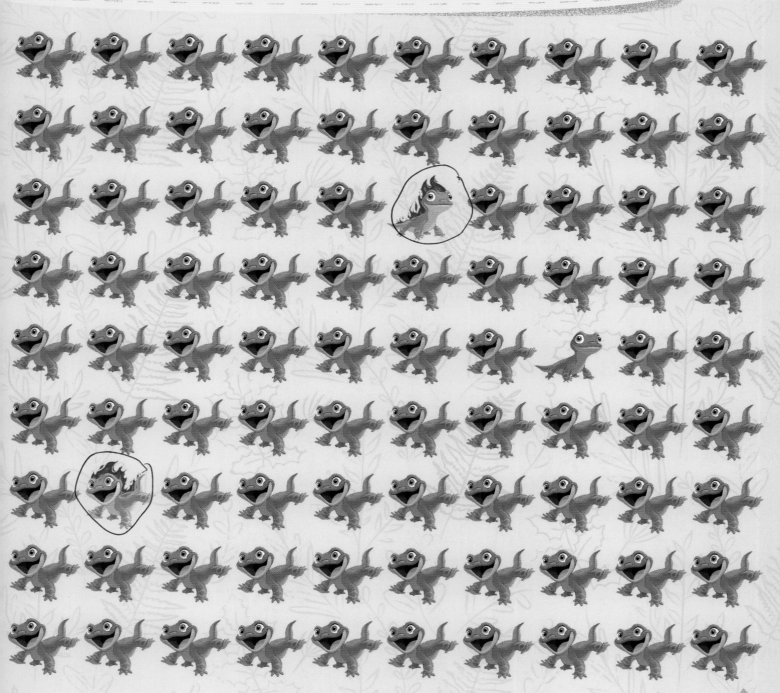

Make Your Own Party Bunting

The castle gates are open and it is nearly time for a party in Arendelle. Can you help with the party prep by making some bunting to decorate the halls?

Ask an adult to help.

You will need:
- Colouring pencils or felt-tip pens
- Scissors
- Ribbon or string
- Sticky tape

How to Make:
- Grab your best pencils or felt-tips and colour in one side of the bunting flags. There is a different design on the back of each flag so you can choose to mix and match.
- Ask an adult to help you carefully cut out each flag. Now line up the flags in any order.
- Cut a length of ribbon or string. Make sure it is a bit longer than the row of bunting flags.
- Use sticky tape to attach the back of each flag to the line of ribbon or string.
- Now hang up your bunting and get the party started!

Stay Safe!
Always ask a grown-up for help when using scissors.

Snow Vs. Stars

It's game on! Anna and Elsa loved to make up fun games when they were young. Challenge somebody in your family to a super sparkly game of Snow Vs. Stars.

How to Play:

- One player draws snowballs, and one player draws stars.
- Take it in turns to draw a snowball or a star in one square.
- The first person to get three in a row, across, down or diagonally, is the winner!

Draw a snowball like this:

○

Draw a star like this:

✳

1

2

3

4

63

Crack the Puzzle

Boom! The Earth Giants have cracked the forest ground. Can you put this shattered puzzle back together again? Write the matching numbers in the spaces or draw the pieces back into the puzzle.

Answers on page 69.

Crystal Count

Elsa is making a magical crystal display for the people of Arendelle. Count the different types of crystals and write down your answers.

I can count ...

0 1 2 3 4 5 6 7 8 9 10

Answers on page 69.

Which Friend Are You?

Have you ever wondered which Frozen friend you are most like? Are you loveable like Olaf, mysterious like Elsa or adventurous like Anna? Take the quiz to find out.

1 What is your favourite colour?

a) blue   b) green   c) yellow

2 What would be your perfect snow day?

b) making a snowman

a) making ice sculptures

c) having a snowball fight

3 What is your favourite weather?

a) ice and snow   b) rainbows   c) sunny!

4 What do you like to do on lazy days?

Party List
1. Invite friends
2. Have fun!

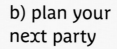

a) go for a walk in nature

b) plan your next party

c) read a book

5 What sentence best describes you?

a) always be true to yourself

b) bah ... who wants to be perfect anyway?

c) warm hugs make everything better!

Mostly As

You are Elsa

You are a shining star! Happy to take your time and think things through, you are careful, thoughtful and true to yourself. The ultimate leader!

6 Where would you most like to have a party?

a) in an ice palace

b) a picnic

c) at the beach

Mostly Bs

You are Anna

You are fun, fun, fun and do everything at top speed. Relax and chill? No way! Not when there are problems to solve and people to help. The ultimate adventurer!

7 Which words are all about you?

a) **quiet** but **strong**

b) **caring** and **brave**

c) **funny** and **kind**

Mostly Cs

You are Olaf

Your happy, sunny self makes everyone smile. You are curious about the world, and always wow your friends with super cool facts. Everyone loves you for being you!

Girl Power

Honeymaren, Elsa and Anna are a force of strength. Copy the colours to make a powerful poster.

Brave
and Bold

68

Answers

Page 11 *Make a Change*
e is the odd one out.

Page 13 *Nature is Magic*
Bruni – FIRE
Giant – EARTH
Nokk – WATER
Gale – WIND

Page 20 *A New World*

Page 22 *Best Buds*
3 and 4 are matching.

Page 25 *Troll Trails*

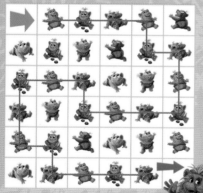

Page 27 *True or False?*
1. False   2. False
3. True   4. False
5. True   6. False
7. False   8. True
9. True   10. False

Page 29 *Winter Wonderland*

Page 38
Castle Designs

Page 44 *Secret Shadows*
1 – d, 2 – c, 3 – a, 4 – e, 5 – b.

Page 45 *Blowing a Gale*

Page 46 *Group Chat*
Kristoff – Reindeer are better than people.
Olaf – Some people are worth melting for.
Elsa – Let it go! Let it go!
Anna – Do you want to build a snowman?

Page 51 *Trust Your Journey*

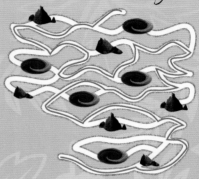

Page 59 *So Many Brunis!*

Page 64 *Crack the Puzzle*

Page 65 *Crystal Count*

 10   8   6

69